Acting Edition

Wish You Were Here

by Sanaz Toossi

|| SAMUEL FRENCH ||

Copyright © 2022 by Sanaz Toossi
All Rights Reserved

WISH YOU WERE HERE is fully protected under the copyright laws
of the United States of America, the British Commonwealth, including
Canada, and all member countries of the Berne Convention for the
Protection of Literary and Artistic Works, the Universal Copyright
Convention, and/or the World Trade Organization conforming to the
Agreement on Trade Related Aspects of Intellectual Property Rights. All
rights, including professional and amateur stage productions, recitation,
lecturing, public reading, motion picture, radio broadcasting, television,
online/digital production, and the rights of translation into foreign
languages are strictly reserved.

ISBN 978-0-573-70987-6

www.concordtheatricals.com
www.concordtheatricals.co.uk

FOR PRODUCTION INQUIRIES

UNITED STATES AND CANADA
info@concordtheatricals.com
1-866-979-0447

UNITED KINGDOM AND EUROPE
licensing@concordtheatricals.co.uk
020-7054-7298

Each title is subject to availability from Concord Theatricals Corp.,
depending upon country of performance. Please be aware that *WISH
YOU WERE HERE* may not be licensed by Concord Theatricals Corp.
in your territory. Professional and amateur producers should contact
the nearest Concord Theatricals Corp. office or licensing partner to
verify availability.

CAUTION: Professional and amateur producers are hereby warned that
WISH YOU WERE HERE is subject to a licensing fee. The purchase,
renting, lending or use of this book does not constitute a license to
perform this title(s), which license must be obtained from Concord
Theatricals Corp. prior to any performance. Performance of this
title(s) without a license is a violation of federal law and may subject
the producer and/or presenter of such performances to civil penalties.
Both amateurs and professionals considering a production are strongly
advised to apply to the appropriate agent before starting rehearsals,
advertising, or booking a theatre. A licensing fee must be paid whether
the title(s) is presented for charity or gain and whether or not admission
is charged. Professional/Stock licensing fees are quoted upon application
to Concord Theatricals Corp.

This work is published by Samuel French, an imprint of Concord
Theatricals Corp.

No one shall make any changes in this title(s) for the purpose of production. No part of this book may be reproduced, stored in a retrieval system, scanned, uploaded, or transmitted in any form, by any means, now known or yet to be invented, including mechanical, electronic, digital, photocopying, recording, videotaping, or otherwise, without the prior written permission of the publisher. No one shall share this title(s), or any part of this title(s), through any social media or file hosting websites.

For all inquiries regarding motion picture, television, online/digital and other media rights, please contact Concord Theatricals Corp.

MUSIC AND THIRD-PARTY MATERIALS USE NOTE

Licensees are solely responsible for obtaining formal written permission from copyright owners to use copyrighted music and/or other copyrighted third-party materials (e.g., artworks, logos) in the performance of this play and are strongly cautioned to do so. If no such permission is obtained by the licensee, then the licensee must use only original music and materials that the licensee owns and controls. Licensees are solely responsible and liable for clearances of all third-party copyrighted materials, including without limitation music, and shall indemnify the copyright owners of the play(s) and their licensing agent, Concord Theatricals Corp., against any costs, expenses, losses and liabilities arising from the use of such copyrighted third-party materials by licensees. For music, please contact the appropriate music licensing authority in your territory for the rights to any incidental music.

IMPORTANT BILLING AND CREDIT REQUIREMENTS

If you have obtained performance rights to this title, please refer to your licensing agreement for important billing and credit requirements.

WISH YOU WERE HERE premiered Off-Broadway at Playwright Horizons' Peter Jay Sharp Theater in New York City on April 12, 2022. The production was directed by Gaye Taylor Upchurch, with scenic design by Arnulfo Maldonado, costume design by Sarah Laux, lighting design by Reza Behjat, sound design by Sinan Refik Zafar and Brian Hickey, and original music by Brandon Terzic. The production stage manager was Vanessa Coakley, and the assistant stage manager was Kayla Owen. The cast was as follows:

NAZANIN	Marjan Neshat
SALME	Roxanna Hope Radja
ZARI	Nikki Massoud
SHIDEH	Artemis Pebdani
RANA	Nazanin Nour

Playwrights Horizons, Inc. New York City produced the World Premiere of *Wish You Were Here* in 2022.

Wish You Were Here was produced by the Williamstown Theatre Festival (Mandy Greenfield, Artistic Director) in collaboration with Audible, released April 2021.

CHARACTERS

All women. All start around age twenty in 1978.

NAZANIN – / ˈnɑːzæniːn / sort of mean

SALME – / ˈsælmɛ / the peacemaker

ZARI – / ˈzæɾi / happy-go-lucky

SHIDEH – / ˈʃidɛ / a little uptight

RANA – / ˈɾænɑː / the queen of cool

NEW FRIEND – played by Shideh

TIME / PLACE

Living rooms in Karaj, Iran from 1978 to 1991

AUTHOR'S NOTE

A slash indicates overlapping dialogue.

1: Salme's Wedding

(1978. Karaj, Iran. A living room.)

(A wedding day! But not a chaotic one.)

(Prep items are strewn about the room.)

(A radio plays Iranian pop.*)

*(Five **WOMEN** get ready for a wedding.)*

*(All look ready except for **RANA**, whose hair is done, but she wears silk pajamas.)*

(A cigarette hangs out of her mouth.)

*(**SALME**, the bride, is wearing a snow beast of a wedding dress.)*

*(She is reading a book, in another world, as **RANA** does her hair.)*

*(**NAZANIN** sits at the foot of **SALME**'s dress with a needle and thread, fixing a tear.)*

*(**ZARI**'s legs hang off the armrest of a couch.)*

(She looks like she is on muscle relaxers. She is not.)

*(**SHIDEH** files **ZARI**'s toenails with great intensity.)*

---

*A license to produce *Wish You Were Here* does not include a performance license for any third-party or copyrighted music. Licensees should create an original composition or use music in the public domain. For further information, please see the Music and Third-Party Materials Use Note on page iii.

RANA. *(To* **SALME.***)* Bobby pin.

NAZANIN. When are you getting dressed?

RANA. I'm almost done. Give me a bigger one. Salme. Salme.

SALME. Hm?

NAZANIN.
I'll get it. Big or small?

SHIDEH.
Zari, your toes are disgusting.

RANA.
Small. Wait. Yeah, small. Salme *khanoom, khoobi*?

ZARI.
I know. I'm sorry.

SALME.
Um.

SHIDEH.
They are hideous. Why is this toe so long?
Aren't you embarrassed?

RANA.
Nervous?

ZARI.
I am embarrassed.

SALME.
A little.

SHIDEH.
You're not embarrassed enough. I'm gonna throw up.

RANA.
A little's good.

ZARI.
Don't throw up.

SALME.
I think so, too.
I'm not even. Really nervous.

SHIDEH.
I'm throwing up.

ZARI. Don't be nervous, Salme!

RANA. Alright you little bitch, stay in your own conversation.

SHIDEH. *Hey.*

RANA. I'm kidding!

SHIDEH. Don't call her that.

RANA. Oh my god it was a joke. She's laughing –

ZARI. I'm laughing!

RANA. Turn the fan this way –

SHIDEH. You can have it when I'm done.

RANA. *(Fanning her vagina.)* Shideh, I'm practically geysering.

SHIDEH. Disgusting.

RANA. I could shoot off into space at any moment.

SHIDEH. And I hope you do. Bon voyage –

RANA. I could hover over that plant and water it right now my god –

SHIDEH. Stop it okay don't bring the plants into this –

NAZANIN. I'm steaming out of my dress, Shideh.

SHIDEH. Ew.

NAZANIN. My pussy could iron a shirt.

RANA. *Oh* what kind of shirt?

NAZANIN. Just like a regular one –

RANA. Oh my god a whole regular shirt, Shideh!

> *(**ZARI** starts stuffing her bra.)*

> *(**SHIDEH** snatches the tissue from her.)*

NAZANIN. My puss-puss, Shideh.

RANA. Her puss-puss, Shideh.

SHIDEH. Well, how about you think of my – *that*.

RANA. You don't even like to think of yours.

ZARI. I like to think / of yours!

RANA. You can't even say it and you're a doctor.

SHIDEH. I'm not a doctor yet.

RANA. Share the fan, Shideh.

NAZANIN. Share the fan.

SHIDEH. You know what, take it up with Salme. She wanted a summer wedding.

SALME. Hm?

RANA. Nothing.

NAZANIN. Shideh said you have great taste.

SALME. *(Moved.)* Oh. Shideh.

SHIDEH. Salme, Zari needs a pumice stone.

ZARI.	SALME.
No, I don't. No, I don't.	Bathroom.

SHIDEH. Which bathroom?

SALME. The *toilet farangi* bathroom.

> (**SHIDEH** *accidentally kicks a shoe while exiting.*)

SHIDEH. Whoever put these shoes here is an idiot.

RANA. *Akhay bebakhshid.*

> (**SHIDEH** *exits.*)

> (**RANA** *moves the fan toward her and* **NAZANIN.**)

RANA. Naz Banu. What am I thinking?

NAZANIN. Um.

RANA. What am I thinking? One.

NAZANIN. Two.

RANA.	**NAZANIN.**
When you tripped over those sandals –	Your mom's high heels!

NAZANIN. *Oh.* Duh. Okay, one.

RANA. Two.

RANA.	**NAZANIN.**
Blisters.	Bunions.

RANA. One.

NAZANIN. Two.

RANA.	**NAZANIN.**
Fallen arches.	Ballerinas.

RANA. Okay I *swear* I was thinking ballerinas –

(**SHIDEH** *enters with a pumice stone.*)

ZARI. Shideh, one –

SHIDEH. No, that game is fucking stupid.

NAZANIN. Leave her feet alone!

SHIDEH. She's going husband-shopping.

NAZANIN. So?

SHIDEH. So if a man saw her toes, I think his penis would fall off.

RANA. Lick them, Shideh. Zari's feet.

SHIDEH. You lick them.

RANA. Let's say one American dollar for each toe.

SHIDEH. Don't be cheap, Rana. I know the conversion rate.

RANA. But if the price is right...

SHIDEH. Maybe. I really want a pool one day.

ZARI. Shideh. Suck my toes for free.

NAZANIN. Doctors do things like this.

ZARI. You know what –

> (**ZARI** *licks her own foot.*)
>
> (*The group reacts in horror.*)

That felt incredible.

RANA. Oh my god. You are so stupid.

SHIDEH. She's not stupid. She's curious and some girls –
they grow up – and they're curious.

> (**NAZANIN** *pokes* **SALME** *with the needle.*
> **SALME** *winces.*)

NAZANIN. Salme. I'm so sorry.

SALME. It's okay.

SHIDEH. What did you do?

NAZANIN. I poked her. Shideh, you don't need to come
over here – Are you okay?

SHIDEH. There are serious arteries down there.

ZARI. Shideh, you're gonna be such a good doctor.

RANA. Salme is fine, everybody is fine. Except for me. Silk
does not breathe well. Whatever you're smelling is me
and I don't want to talk about it. What do you think,
khanoom?

> (**SALME** *looks at herself in the mirror.*)

SALME. The dress is very big, isn't it?

SHIDEH.   **ZARI.**
  It's a proper dress.   It's so pretty!

RANA.
You look like a fucking queen.

NAZANIN.
The Queen of Karaj.

SALME. You can barely see me.

ZARI. I can see you!

RANA. You are *extremely* visible.

SALME. Does my head look tiny?

NAZANIN. No.

RANA. *No.*

ZARI. What do you mean by tiny?

SHIDEH. A dress should be big in a way that sort of feels humiliating.

SALME. Should a dress feel / humiliating?

NAZANIN. You look powerful.

RANA. Yes. *Yes.*

NAZANIN. You look – you're like –

RANA. You're like a sexy avalanche victim.

NAZANIN. Exactly.

RANA. *(Patting SALME's breast.)* And the smaller your head looks, the bigger your boobs look.

NAZANIN. *(Patting SALME's other breast.)* We should find ways to make your head look even smaller.

ZARI. Salme, have you ever ridden a horse?

RANA. Don't answer that.

SALME. No. Why?

ZARI. Okay, I... Should I tell her?

SHIDEH. Tell her. She should know.

ZARI. It's gonna hurt tonight.

SHIDEH. When you anatomically merge –

NAZANIN. Jesus.

SHIDEH. Oh my god do you think I just made that up? I'm
not a fucking pervert –

RANA.

You have nothing to be
afraid of.

NAZANIN.

You're freaking her out.

SHIDEH. You don't know that.

ZARI. Have you ever seen one, Salme?

SALME. Seen what?

NAZANIN. She's asking if you've seen a penis.

ZARI. A man's penis. The penis of a man.

SALME. *Oh* uh no.

ZARI. Call me when you do.

SALME. Totally.

RANA. There's a vein. That's all you need to know.

ZARI. A vein?

RANA. I know.

ZARI. Why?

RANA. It's unclear.

ZARI. That makes me so sad.

RANA. I understand.

SHIDEH. Hold on. When did you see one, Rana?

RANA. It was by accident.

SHIDEH. A-ha. Okay.

RANA. God, Shideh.

SHIDEH. Are you thinking of one right now?

ZARI. When you first see one, smile. Smile so big. Smile bigger than you've ever smiled in your life. Like you need to swallow a plate.

SHIDEH. Show her.

(**ZARI** *demonstrates.*)

Did you want to see that again, Salme?

RANA. Okay, you're not allowed to talk to Salme anymore.

NAZANIN. It's okay. He might not be able to find your vagine under all of this.

SALME. Really?

NAZANIN. Does that make you feel better?

SALME. Yeah. I think it does.

NAZANIN. Oh good yeah I really don't think he's gonna find it –

SALME. Do I smell?

RANA. You smell great.

SALME. No does it smell.

RANA. Does what smell?

SALME. *It.*

NAZANIN. She thinks her pussy stinks.

RANA. Oh, Salme, you want a pussy audit?

SALME. Yes. Do you mind.

RANA. It's your day. We'll smell whatever you need us to smell. Let me get down here –

SHIDEH. That is not a good idea. No. *No.*

(**NAZANIN** *helps* **SALME** *lift her dress.*)

(**RANA** *disappears under it.*)

SALME. Be honest.

RANA. Yeah.

SHIDEH. Breathe through your mouth.

RANA. *Bah bah.*

NAZANIN. See! It's good!

SALME. I don't know. Do you have perfume?

SHIDEH. Give it a spritz down there. Maybe two.

RANA. No spritzing. *No spritzing.*

SHIDEH. There comes a time in a woman's life when soap doesn't cut it.

    And I think it was really brave of me to say that just now.

SALME. I'm just nervous –

SHIDEH. Well, it's gonna hurt. Zari's right.

RANA. *Stop it* –

SALME. No Shideh's right it's okay –

SHIDEH. You'll be okay. Even though it hurts so much God must be punishing you.

NAZANIN.	RANA.
Don't listen to Shideh.	*It will feel good.*

SHIDEH. Won't feel good tonight.

RANA. Yes it will.

SHIDEH. No it won't.

RANA. Whatever *god* they don't tell us anything about anything.

SHIDEH. Rana Rana Rana there is ash on her dress –

RANA. Oh, shit. My bad.

SHIDEH. Should you really be smoking?

RANA. Why?

SHIDEH. Salme doesn't smoke.

RANA. Salme *khanoom*, can I smoke?

SALME. Sure.

RANA. Do you want a cigarette? To relax?

SALME. Should I?

RANA. Yes. Duh. Fucking duh you should. Here.

SHIDEH. You're gonna *smell*.

RANA. The men smell.

>   (**SHIDEH** *coughs.*)

NAZANIN. Why are *you* coughing?

SALME. Are you / okay?

RANA. I am in no way convinced by this cough.

SHIDEH. I'm gonna puke.

RANA. Well, do it over there. By Zari.

SHIDEH. It's so fucking hot. I'm gonna pass out.

ZARI. Shideh, come have a puke.

SALME. Shideh?

SHIDEH. What?

SALME. Come here for a second.

SHIDEH. Why?

SALME. One second. Come here.

>   (**SHIDEH** *goes to* **SALME**.)

>   (**SALME** *hugs* **SHIDEH**.)

(She holds on for a long time.)

(Everyone watches. Still holding **SHIDEH***:)*

SALME. Are you applying to medical school?

SHIDEH. Yeah.

SALME. That's exciting.

SHIDEH. Not really.

SALME. I wish you were my doctor.

(Beat.)

SHIDEH. I'm trying to fast-track my diploma. In case.

SALME. Of what?

SHIDEH. I don't know. The protests. Everything. And the –
there's static in the air.

SALME. I think you're gonna get in everywhere you apply.

SHIDEH. *Cheshmam nazan.*

SALME. Can't jinx God's will.

SHIDEH. Yes, I can. I could do that.

SALME. Where do you want to go?

SHIDEH. I don't want to say it out loud.

SALME. Can you tell me? In my ear?

*(***SHIDEH*** whispers in* **SALME***'s ear.)*

NAZANIN. *(To* **ZARI***.)* Where?

ZARI. Shiraz Pahlavi.

SHIDEH. *Are you fucking serious?*

ZARI. I'm sorry. I'm / so sorry.

NAZANIN. That was my fault. I asked –

SHIDEH. Could you *not*?

SALME. You're getting in.

SHIDEH. Stop.

SALME. I just like, can feel it.

SHIDEH. Okayokayokay.

SALME. I'd bet my life on it right now.

SHIDEH. *Salme shut up.*

SALME. You're getting in.

> (*Beat.*)

SHIDEH. Am I ruining your wedding?

SALME. No.

RANA. Yes.

SALME. *No –*

SHIDEH. I'm sorry. I have a yeast infection. Can everyone tell? I'm sorry.

SALME. I can't tell.

SHIDEH. I can't stop getting yeast infections.

SALME. I really can't tell.

> (**SHIDEH** *melts into* **SALME**'s *hug.*)
>
> (*Then* **SALME** *lets* **SHIDEH** *go, kissing her on the cheek.*)
>
> (*This has calmed everyone.*)

NAZANIN. Your hem's fixed, *aroos khanoom.*

RANA. *Be eftekhare Naz Banu.*

> (*The* **WOMEN** *celebrate.*)

RANA. *Aroos bayad beraghse!*

ALL. *Aroos bayad beraghse!*

(**SALME** *trips on her dress.*)

(*The* **WOMEN** *shriek.*)

SHIDEH. Okay, let's not. Let's really not. Playtime's over.

(**SALME, ZARI,** *and* **SHIDEH** *move into a conversation.*)

RANA. This shit is so embarrassing.

NAZANIN. I know.

RANA. Please never get married.

NAZANIN. Okay.

RANA. Please never have children.

NAZANIN. I won't. If you won't.

RANA. Thank you.

NAZANIN. Say you won't.

RANA. I won't. So what's our plan?

NAZANIN. You graduate, I graduate and we move to Tehran. Amirabad.

RANA. Mmm –

NAZANIN. Okay – Zaferaniye. Into one of those newer buildings.

RANA. Naz Banu. No.

NAZANIN. Okay. Then...Miami.

RANA. Miami. Okay. And that is...

NAZANIN. It's a city in Florida.

RANA. Okay.

NAZANIN. On the water.

RANA. Amazing.

NAZANIN. Near Comrade Fidel.

RANA. *Rafiqe mun.*

NAZANIN. And. Are you ready. This is big.

RANA. I'm ready.

NAZANIN. Jews.

RANA. Jews? Who are Jewish?

NAZANIN. Jews who are Jewish.

RANA. Like me?

NAZANIN. Like you.

RANA. Oh my god.

NAZANIN. This is a real place.

RANA. I believe you. I always believe you.

NAZANIN. But. No judging.

RANA. Okay.

NAZANIN. No judging.

RANA. *Be khoda* no judging.

NAZANIN. I want to come back.

RANA. Here?

NAZANIN. Eventually.

RANA. Why?

NAZANIN. I don't know. I just do.

RANA. Okay. Yeah. Let's come back.

SHIDEH. Look at these two. Barf.

RANA. Shideh, hold on. Bend over.

SHIDEH. Why?

RANA. There's *wow* there's a – huge stick up your ass. Do you want me to get it for you?

SALME. Rana, can we try it with the *roosari*?

RANA. Yeah.

> (**RANA** *retrieves a white, silk hijab.*)

Naz Banu, hold this.

> (**NAZANIN** *and* **RANA** *drape the hijab around* **SALME**'s *head.*)

SALME. Wait. Oh.

RANA. What?

SALME. Rana. It's noon. I forgot.

RANA. No. Salme. I'm serious. No.

SALME.	**ZARI.**
It slipped my mind.	Wait. What's happening?

SHIDEH. Did you not think about this?

SALME. I can't pray in the dress. It'll be quick.

RANA. It's never quick. It's designed to be like, inconveniently long.

SHIDEH. That's true. That's on purpose.

RANA. God will forgive you. You look really pretty *mashallah* and He cares about that kind of thing.

NAZANIN. Do you have to?

SALME. Today of all days. I have to. Or else I'm like, jinxing my marriage.

RANA. You said jinxing's not real.

SALME. I said you can't jinx your destiny.

RANA. So it's not your destiny to get married.

SALME. That's not what I said.

RANA. It is what you said.

SALME. Don't you ask God for things?

RANA. Not really.

SALME. Then who do you ask?

RANA. Nazy.

SALME. Sure. Yeah.

> (**RANA** *licks* **NAZANIN** *on the cheek.*)

RANA. Everyone take a side.

> (*They gather around* **SALME**'s *dress.*)

Nazy, get her zipper. Okay, gentle. *Gentle.*

SHIDEH. *(To* **ZARI**.) *Gentle.*

ZARI. Very gentle.

RANA. Alright, you little bitch, are you ready?

SALME. Yes.

> (*Slowly, all together, they lift* **SALME**'s *dress off of her.*)

2: Zari's Wedding

(1979.)

(Clothes, makeup, shoes – they have exploded everywhere.)

(It's **ZARI***'s wedding day.)*

*(***ZARI***, too, is in a massive wedding dress, but she loves it.)*

(Four **WOMEN** *now:* **NAZANIN, ZARI, SHIDEH,** *and* **SALME** *are all wedding-ready. No* **RANA***.)*

*(***SALME** *is reading a book, smoking, oblivious to the chaos around her.)*

*(***NAZANIN** *is mending* **ZARI***'s veil.)*

*(***SHIDEH** *plucks* **ZARI***'s eyebrows.)*

SHIDEH. Wow, who told women it was a good idea to fill in their eyebrows?

ZARI. Googoosh fills in her eyebrows –

SHIDEH. Googoosh doesn't have your uncle's eyebrows.

ZARI. Do I look like my uncle?

NAZANIN. No!

SHIDEH. She doesn't not look like her uncle –

ZARI. My uncle wishes he could look this hot.

NAZANIN. I need another pin. Salme.

SHIDEH. God, speak up. *Salme.*

SALME. Hm?

NAZANIN. I need a pin –

ZARI. Waitwait how will I pee in this?

NAZANIN. It's unclear.

ZARI. Salme, how did you pee?

SALME. I didn't.

ZARI. How am I getting out of this tonight?

NAZANIN. Your mother-in-law will help you.

ZARI. *What.*

SALME. She's kidding.

SHIDEH. She'll be holding your hand every step of the way.

ZARI. Good. She can watch me enjoy it.

SHIDEH. You won't enjoy it.

ZARI. Yes, I will –

NAZANIN. Yes, she will –

ZARI. Salme?

SALME. Of course you will.

ZARI. How will it feel?

SALME. Okay. Yeah. It's...

NAZANIN. ...Sounds amazing.

ZARI. Oh god.

SHIDEH. You'll be fine. You've slid down a lot of bannisters in your day.

NAZANIN. Pin.

ZARI. Another one?

NAZANIN. Stop moving –

ZARI. Salme, how did you get out of your dress?

SHIDEH. Yes, how does one exit a cream puff, Salme?

SALME.	NAZANIN.
You don't look like a cream puff!	She doesn't look like a cream puff.

(**SHIDEH** *wets her finger and dabs* **ZARI**'s *eyebrows.*)

ZARI.	NAZANIN.
Stop!	Don't touch her makeup!

ZARI. I just want one day where I make other girls feel ugly.

SALME. Of course.

NAZANIN. You will.

SALME. You look amazing.

NAZANIN. Other girls will be devastated. They're going to feel really bad.

SALME. You're going to be the prettiest girl in the room.

SHIDEH. Oh yeah.

ZARI. Thank you.

SHIDEH. There are gonna be a lot of hideous people at this wedding.

(**ZARI** *swats* **SHIDEH**'s *butt.*)

SHIDEH. That was a reassurance!

ZARI. No, it wasn't.

SHIDEH. What? My family's gonna be there, too.

ZARI. You're in a mood. Are you on your period?

SHIDEH. Why? Because I have an *opinion*?

SALME. Have you heard from the American schools, Shideh?

SHIDEH. Not yet.

SALME. You will.

SHIDEH. I fucking better. *What*, Nazanin?

NAZANIN. What?

SHIDEH. You know we can *see* you when you roll your eyes.

NAZANIN. I think it's a little silly to go all that way knowing you're gonna come back.

SHIDEH. You should think about it.

NAZANIN. Think about what?

SHIDEH. *Engineering* programs abroad.

NAZANIN. You're bringing negativity into the room.

SHIDEH. Oh no oh no there's so much negativity go away negativity we hate you –

NAZANIN. Whatever.

SHIDEH. The Shah just *left*, Nazanin.

NAZANIN. Well.

SHIDEH. He just like, got up and left.

NAZANIN. This will all blow over in a year.

ZARI. I had a dream my boobs got so big I fell off a cliff.

SALME. That's a good omen.

ZARI. I hope it comes true.

SHIDEH. Auspicious.

ZARI. Listen, your deflowering will come one day, Shideh. Hang in there.

SHIDEH. Get off me.

ZARI. Actually are you a virgin / technically –

NAZANIN. Shideh?!

SHIDEH. *I am still a virgin.*

ZARI. Letting him in through the back door is not the loophole you think it is –

SHIDEH.   **NAZANIN.**
   Zari come on.   Oh my god.

ZARI. Shideh's a butt girl.

SHIDEH. You know what, whatever. I'm still a virgin.

ZARI.   **NAZANIN.**
   Are you?   No. You're not. Salme, do
                                      you want to chime in?

SALME. You know, I'm not really an / expert on –

SHIDEH. Am I still a virgin, Salme?

          (Beat.)

SALME. Shideh, your eyes are so pretty.

NAZANIN. That's a no.

SALME. I didn't say that!

SHIDEH. You know what, get up. I can't do hair as fast as Rana and your makeup is – get up, get up.

          (Rana's name changes the air.)

          (ZARI gathers her dress and sits.)

          (SHIDEH fusses with her hair.)

          (NAZANIN mends ZARI's veil.)

ZARI. Did you have to say her name?

SHIDEH. What do you want me to call her? The cool Jewish girl we used to hang out / with?

ZARI. No, I know.

SHIDEH. She's fine.

ZARI. How do you know?

SHIDEH. Why the fuck am I standing here? I don't do hair. Nazanin, *biya inja.*

ZARI. Why did you say she's fine?

SHIDEH. I don't know. It's just something I said.

ZARI. Did you talk to her? Did she call you?

SHIDEH. Why would Rana call me? She'd call Nazy or Salme.

SALME. She'd call you, Shideh. You were her friend.

ZARI. *Is* her friend.

SALME. She would call you.

SHIDEH. Whatever, you know what I mean.

ZARI. No one's seen her parents yet, right?

That's – That's probably a good sign –

You know, like, they all left at once.

SHIDEH. A family of Jews going missing is usually not a good sign –

ZARI. Okay. Okay. Please stop talking. I'm sorry I asked.

(**ZARI** *sighs. The mood is forlorn.*)

(**SHIDEH** *panics and:*)

SHIDEH. Salme's looking for her.

ZARI. Really?

SALME. Oh – I mean – sort of –

ZARI. Do you know where she is?

SALME. No –

ZARI. Salme. I have goosebumps. You're gonna find her.

SALME. Well, I'm just going through – I'm asking around. I made a list of everyone she knew or mentioned in passing / or –

ZARI. Let me see.

SALME. It's in my purse but don't – don't – please don't get your hopes up –

SHIDEH. They're up. It's too late. Is this your purse –

ZARI. Salme, cute purse!

SHIDEH. Focus.

ZARI. Sorry.

> (**SALME** *hands* **SHIDEH** *a list.*)
>
> (**SHIDEH** *and* **ZARI** *look over it.*)

Who is Agha Kashani?

SHIDEH. Oh this guy this guy who almost died choking on a walnut –

ZARI. Very publicly –

SHIDEH.

Publicly choking on a walnut.	**ZARI.**
Kill yourself.	Yeah.

SALME. Their apartment looks unbothered.

There were dishes in the sink.

ZARI. *You snuck in?*

SHIDEH. *You broke into her home?*

SALME. I know where the spare is so I climbed the fence –

SHIDEH. The *fence*?!

ZARI. Salme, oh my god –

SALME. Nothing was missing. That's good, isn't it?

> (*Beat.*)

SHIDEH. No signs of a struggle. It's a good thing. Definitely.

Next time, you're – nevermind. Nevermind.

SALME. What?

SHIDEH. No, it's stupid.

SALME. Tell me.

SHIDEH. If you go back, I just – okay, honestly, she took a lot of pens from me over the years and I would like some of them back.

ZARI. Why didn't you tell me you were looking for her?

SHIDEH. Does the list look complete to you, Nazanin? Do you want to look again?

NAZANIN. I haven't looked.

SHIDEH. *(Offering it to her.)* Well, here.

NAZANIN. No.

SHIDEH. You're not worried about her?

NAZANIN. She's not dead.

SHIDEH. How would you know?

NAZANIN. She's just not. I would know.

SHIDEH. Oh, you think you're psychic? Bitches love to think they're psychic.

SALME. I believe you. I think you would know.

ZARI. Don't you want to be sure?

NAZANIN. She knows my phone number by heart. If she wanted to vanish into thin air, with no trace, no word, without shit, then that's how she wanted to do it.

SHIDEH. Take one look at this list –

NAZANIN. Whoever I know, Salme knows.

ZARI. But you knew that side of her dad's family and there was that study group she joined –

NAZANIN. I remember everything about her, Zari.

(Beat.)

ZARI. Okay. Well.

Okay.

NAZANIN. Okay.

*(The list is returned to **SALME**.)*

*(**ZARI** tries to apply glue on her false eyelashes.)*

ZARI. Lashes.

SHIDEH. No, I'm not doing that.

ZARI. Salme, how did you get these on?

NAZANIN. Rana did them for her. I'll do it.

ZARI. Thank you.

NAZANIN. Mhm.

*(**NAZANIN** dabs glue onto the eyelashes.)*

*(**SHIDEH** watches closely.)*

SHIDEH. That's a lot of glue.

God, you are sweating.

NAZANIN. Thank you, Shideh. I was really hoping you'd bring it up.

SHIDEH. Any time.

*(**NAZANIN** tries to put the lashes on **ZARI**.)*

Okay, that's her lash. Don't glue it onto her *actual lash, Nazanin –*

NAZANIN. *Shideh, two steps back.* No, another. Go water the plant.

SHIDEH. If you rip off her eyelashes, Jamshid will divorce her in the morning.

NAZANIN. If you end up in the States, you are 100 percent getting deported.

SHIDEH. Why would I get deported?

NAZANIN. For being annoying.

SHIDEH. Oh, okay. You saw *Grease* twice and now you're an expert on American culture. *Don't attach them to her eyelashes –*

NAZANIN. Zari, you don't need these. I'm sorry.

ZARI. It's okay!

SALME. This is better.

ZARI. This is way better.

NAZANIN. Okay.

SALME. You'll look more like yourself in your wedding photographs –

NAZANIN. Salme.

SALME. What? She'll have children one day.

NAZANIN. You don't know that.

ZARI. I'm getting pregnant tonight.

SALME. See!

SHIDEH. There's that eye roll again! Ooo that was a big one!

SALME. What? Did I say something?

NAZANIN. It's always motherhood with you.

ZARI. Shideh, are you happy for me?

SHIDEH. Well, you reversed on the freeway last week so this is a big day for you.

NAZANIN. You reversed on the freeway?

ZARI. It made sense and I'll probably do it again.

SALME. Totally.

ZARI. Isn't he great?

SHIDEH. Who?

NAZANIN. Shideh.

SHIDEH. Oh! Jamshid? No.

SALME.	**NAZANIN.**
He's perfect.	He's so great.

SHIDEH. Okay, relax. He's fine.

ZARI. Are you gonna have a good day today?

SHIDEH. What?

ZARI. Answer me.

SHIDEH. I don't know.

ZARI. Because I can only have a good day if you have a good day. So are you gonna have a good day?

SHIDEH. Weddings make me sad.

ZARI. Why?

SHIDEH. You'll be gone.

ZARI. I won't be gone. You're the one who's –

SHIDEH. I'm coming back. I am.

ZARI. Good.

SHIDEH. Yeah.

> *(Beat.)*

ZARI. I have to – nevermind.

SHIDEH. What is it?

ZARI. I need to tell you something but no judging.

SHIDEH. Okay. *Be khoda.* Tell me.

(Beat.)

ZARI. I found my clitoris last night.

SHIDEH. Oh. Awesome.

ZARI. Do you want me to help you find yours?

SHIDEH. No thank you.

ZARI. Once you find it you're like duh. Fucking duh. So. Let me know.

SHIDEH. That's very generous. Thank you.

(Beat.)

ZARI. I know it's strange out there, but –

SALME. Today is a good day.

ZARI. And change is good. Right?

NAZANIN.	**SALME.**
Yes. And it's barely – yes.	Yes.

(Beat.)

SHIDEH. Yes.

3: The War

(1980.)

(No wedding. No occasion. In the distance, we hear a siren wail.)

(Three **WOMEN** *now.)*

*(***SALME*** and* **NAZANIN** *play backgammon.)*

*(***ZARI*** hides under a table, terrified.)*

(No **SHIDEH.** *Still no* **RANA.***)*

NAZANIN. Is that cheating?

SALME. I don't think so.

NAZANIN. Yes, it is.

SALME. No, you can't go *here*.

NAZANIN. I did go there.

SALME. Oh. That's cheating.

NAZANIN. Let's start over.

       *(***ZARI*** slams her head against the coffee table.)*

ZARI. *Ow.*

NAZANIN.	**SALME.**
(Laughing.) Oh shit.	Are you okay?

ZARI. *Fuck.*

NAZANIN.	**ZARI.**
That was so loud.	That really, really hurt.

NAZANIN. Yeah, it probably did –

SALME. Are you alright? *(To* **NAZANIN.***)* Could you get ice?

NAZANIN. Oh, man. She probably has a concussion.

ZARI. No, don't go in there. *The glass from the windows could maim you.*

NAZANIN. Oh no.

    *(**NAZANIN** goes to the kitchen.)*

ZARI. Please get under here. Please.

SALME. Um. Okay.

    *(**SALME** crawls under the table.)*

    *(**NAZANIN** returns, still laughing.)*

NAZANIN. Ice is melted. The fridge reeks. *(To **SALME**.)* Where are you going?

    *(**SALME** bumps against the table.)*

    *(This sets **NAZANIN** and **SALME**'s laughter off.)*

SALME. Ow.

NAZANIN. Looks great under there. Very safe. This table murdered my leg last Norooz. Do you remember?

SALME. Yeah that scar on / the –

ZARI. *Nazanin.* There could be a missile hurtling towards us right / now –

NAZANIN.	**SALME.**
There's no missile.	We're safe here.

ZARI. The alarm –

NAZANIN. That alarm couldn't detect a fart.

SALME.	**ZARI.**
True.	Why would it detect farts –

NAZANIN. If we ran to the shelter every time that thing sounded off –

ZARI. There have been missile strikes –

NAZANIN.	SALME.
In Tehran.	But in Tehran.

NAZANIN. Saddam Hussein doesn't care about Karaj.

SALME. Should we go to the shelter?

NAZANIN. The shelters smell like mold and pits and I'd rather die here where it only smells like pits.

ZARI. Is it me? The pit smell?

NAZANIN. ...No.

SALME. Come play.

ZARI. Backgammon is a two-man game.

NAZANIN. Take over for me. I need to study.

ZARI. For what?

NAZANIN. The universities *will* reopen, you know –

ZARI. Oh don't say that. The universities closing is the best thing that's ever happened to me.

NAZANIN. Oh, good. Happy for you. I, for one, hope they reopen.

SALME. They will. I promise.

NAZANIN. You can't promise that.

SALME. Well, here I am promising it to you.

(**ZARI** *emerges from the table.*)

(**NAZANIN** *and* **SALME** *clap and ululate for her.*)

NAZANIN.	SALME.
Welcome to the living room.	Careful!

SALME. Play with me. Nazy's the white.

(**ZARI** *and* **SALME** *play.*)

(**NAZANIN** *retreats to the couch.*)

ZARI. I had a weird dream last night.

SALME. Yeah?

ZARI. Jamshid got drafted. And I had to go with him. So I packed all our bags. But I only brought nail polish.

SALME. I wonder what it means.

NAZANIN. You know who Salme's been having dreams about?

ZARI. Who?

SALME. Oh my god no –

NAZANIN. Saddam Hussein.

ZARI. Oh.

NAZANIN. Have you heard of him, Zari?

SALME. Nazy.

NAZANIN. War-criminal Saddam. Not like, another Saddam. You know the one.

SALME. Okay, I just want to say that in the dream we *are* married –

NAZANIN. Even better – Zari that's cheating –

SALME. Nono that's how we were playing.

NAZANIN. Wish someone knew the rules.

SALME. How is Shideh? Does she like Indiana?

ZARI. I don't know. International calls are very expensive.

SALME. They really are. Has school started?

ZARI. Um, I think so.

NAZANIN. So you haven't really spoken with her?

ZARI. Well, the time difference –

SALME. Let's call from my phone next time.

ZARI. Okay. Yeah.

NAZANIN. I just want to make sure you know which Saddam I'm referring to, Zari –

ZARI. Mustard-gas Saddam. I'm familiar. I really have to pee.

NAZANIN. Well, the water's off. Flush with the water bottle.

ZARI. Ew no.

NAZANIN. Fine, then. Hold it.

SALME. I can't either. It's so gross.

ZARI. Yeah, it's disgusting, isn't it –

NAZANIN. Wait, what am I thinking? One.

SALME. Uh –

NAZANIN. Come on. One.

SALME. Two.

SALME.	**NAZANIN.**
Your dad.	Agha Falla's mustache.

NAZANIN. Oh, Salme. No. You're thinking about my father right now?

SALME. No, I think *you're* thinking about your father –

NAZANIN. Do you associate my father with Saddam Hussein?

SALME. Yeah, but like, in a really positive way –

ZARI. That's not funny.

NAZANIN. Don't interrupt her. Salme, you were saying.

SALME. It's – no, it's stupid –

ZARI. Jamshid could get drafted any day now. What's wrong with you?

NAZANIN. You're right. Salme's making light of pain and death.

ZARI. I just mean it's not funny –

NAZANIN. Well, it's not funny anymore.

Just because there's a war doesn't mean we have to be boring.

(*Beat.*)

Why don't you two just go to the shelter?

SALME.	**ZARI.**
No.	Fine.

SALME. No, no, it's safer here –

ZARI. I'm sure I can dodge any missile coming my way. I'm athletic.

SALME. Nono wait. I have to pray.

ZARI. You already prayed.

SALME. Just quickly. A quick one.

ZARI. Salme, I'm fine.

SALME. Will you give me one second?

ZARI. Sure.

(**SALME** *exits.*)

(**ZARI** *touches* **SALME**'s *prayer.*)

Is this stone from Karbala?

NAZANIN. She says it is.

(*Beat.*)

ZARI. Do you ever think...she's too religious?

NAZANIN. No. Never.

Why would you say that?

(**SALME** *enters with a chador.*)

(She settles onto the prayer rug.)

SALME. Okay.

　　　*(***SALME*** *prays.)*

　　　(When she finishes, she cracks her back.)

NAZANIN. That's my favorite part.

SALME. When I crack my back?

NAZANIN.	**ZARI.**
Yeah.	What'd you pray for?

SALME. The water, the sirens, Shideh.

ZARI. That's nice that you pray for Shideh.

NAZANIN. Why wouldn't she?

ZARI. I don't know. She left, so –

NAZANIN. So we don't know her anymore?

ZARI. Are you serious?

SALME. I – I pray for everyone.

ZARI. Do you pray for Rana?

SALME. Yeah. Everyone.

　　　(Beat.)

ZARI. No judging.

SALME. *Be khoda* no judging.

ZARI. Sometimes I wonder if Shideh's lonely.

And maybe it wouldn't be the worst thing if she is.

NAZANIN. Yikes.

ZARI. I'm – okay, obviously I hope she's okay. Of course.

SALME. Of course.

ZARI. I would never – I'm not – wishing her unhappiness –

I hope everyone's okay. Even Rana – I hope Israel's okay –

NAZANIN. Rana's where?

ZARI. Uh. I. Israel? I don't know.

NAZANIN. Is that a guess or –

ZARI. It's a guess! Just a guess.

NAZANIN. Oh. Okay. A Jew. In Israel. Good work.

SALME. She's not guessing. Her brother is in Israel. She could be there. It's not unlikely.

NAZANIN. Davood or Kazem?

SALME. Davood.

ZARI. Davood. He had. Big hands.

NAZANIN. How do you know all this?

SALME. I'm looking for her.

NAZANIN. Still?

SALME. Of course.

(Beat.)

NAZANIN. Then I hope Israel is a pleasure. I hope she never comes back. I hope she never calls.

SALME. She will call you one day.

NAZANIN. She will not. She's had, what, two years to pick up the phone –

SALME. She will call you.

NAZANIN. Then I will hang up on her.

SALME. You will not.

NAZANIN. I will and I'm already looking forward to it.

SALME. *No you will not.*

NAZANIN. It's going to feel incredible.

> (**NAZANIN** *and* **SALME** *laugh.* **ZARI** *remains left out.*)

ZARI. I think it's nice that you pray for Rana.

SALME. Well, I – there's a lot, I – you know, for Nazy, I pray for a nice man.

ZARI.	**NAZANIN.**
That's a good one.	Don't do that.

ZARI. You don't want to meet a nice man and get married?

NAZANIN. No.

ZARI. What if you fall in love?

NAZANIN. Pray for bigger things.

ZARI. Falling in love isn't big to you?

NAZANIN. Not particularly.

SALME.	**ZARI.**
I don't believe you.	Life is easier with a husband.

NAZANIN. That's not true everywhere.

ZARI. Oh, are you going somewhere?

NAZANIN. I'm just saying that's not always the case.

SALME. Well, I like to wish things for you that you wouldn't wish for yourself –

NAZANIN. Alrightalrightalright shutup.

> (**NAZANIN** *licks* **SALME.**)

SALME. Where are you going?

ZARI. I have to pee.

SALME. Wait, do you have the water bottle?

(ZARI ignores her as she exits.)

(NAZANIN rolls her eyes.)

I won't wish for that if it bothers you.

NAZANIN. They're your wishes.

(Beat.)

Salme, will you do something for me?

SALME. Anything.

NAZANIN. Stop looking for her.

SALME. Why?

NAZANIN. Because she's not here anymore.

Please.

(Beat.)

SALME. Okay.

4: Then There Were Two

(1981.)

(Just two **WOMEN** *now:* **SALME** *and* **NAZANIN***.)*

(A mannequin with the makings of a dress on it stands somewhere.)

(It's raining outside.)

*(***SALME***, who is nervously smoking, waxes* **NAZANIN***'s legs.)*

NAZANIN. Salme, you can't think about it / too much –

SALME. I know –

NAZANIN. Go ahead and pull it. I don't even need a warning.

SALME. Wouldn't a warning help?

NAZANIN. Come on. One, two, say it with me, / one, two...

SALME. One, two...

*(***SALME** *does not pull the strip.)*

NAZANIN. There's ash on my leg –

SALME. It's getting on your leg, oh no, / oh sorry.

NAZANIN. How many of these have you smoked today?

SALME. Too many. I know.

NAZANIN. Try again.

SALME. Doesn't it hurt?

NAZANIN. Yeah it hurts.

SALME. Is shaving not an / option?

NAZANIN. Shaving is not an option for me. I'm not like you. I grow real Iranian hair.

SALME. What does that mean?

NAZANIN. It means my leg hair is pubic hair. Come on. The wax will congeal. Pull it. Ready?

SALME. Okay.

NAZANIN. Count off this time.

SALME. Three, two...

Sorry sorry.

> (**SALME** *stares at the strip.* **NAZANIN** *sighs.*)
>
> (*It sucks the warmth out of the room.*)

NAZANIN. What happened to the sirens?

SALME. It's been a few weeks. Could be a good sign.

NAZANIN. I sort of miss them. The noise of it all.

Noise, as it turns out, is not so bad.

> (**NAZANIN** *tears the strip herself.*)

SALME. Oh god.

NAZANIN. See. *Tamum shod.*

> (**NAZANIN** *prepares the next strip.*)

SALME. Zari won't call me back. I hope she's okay.

NAZANIN. That girl's too dumb to be sad.

SALME. Nazy.

NAZANIN. That's a compliment. I wish I was stupid.

SALME. Have you called her?

NAZANIN. A-ha.

SALME. Oh, really?

NAZANIN. Really.

SALME. I think it'd be more meaningful coming from you.

NAZANIN. She's being pissy for attention. She doesn't deserve you. Stop calling her.

SALME. I kind of get it, though. How she feels.

NAZANIN. How she feels left out?

SALME. Yeah.

NAZANIN. What is there to be left out of? We don't do anything. We don't go anywhere. It's your place, my place or the bomb shelter.

SALME. We play a lot of backgammon.

NAZANIN. God, you feel responsible for everything. Did you start the war?

SALME. No.

NAZANIN. Are you sure?

SALME. Yes. / Yeah.

NAZANIN. And this hostage business...

SALME. Also not me.

NAZANIN. I don't know how you live like this. I would kill myself if I were this nice.

SALME. You're nice.

NAZANIN. You should try being mean. You'd probably sleep better.

SALME. Threes are hard, you know?

NAZANIN. What do you mean?

SALME. I guess when it was – when it was you, me and...

NAZANIN. And Rana?

SALME. Yeah. It's just, sort of natural that someone feels – you know.

NAZANIN. Left out? That's how you felt? With Rana and me?

SALME. Nonono I think I –

And you didn't mean to.

But it could feel like. It was just me.

NAZANIN. I made you feel alone?

(*Beat.*)

That's the worst thing I've ever heard.

SALME. No judging.

NAZANIN. Okay.

SALME. I like it this way. The two of us.

I like being your first call. I like being your only audience.

I sort of revel in the thought that you might love me more than anyone else.

I know you didn't mean to make me feel alone. You would never do that.

NAZANIN. I would. I did. With Zari.

You're normal, Salme. But I um. I think I light up when I make someone feel that way.

But I would never do that to you.

(*Beat.*)

Do you think Rana knew?

SALME. Um.

NAZANIN. Yeah I think she did, too.

SALME. Maybe I'll tell Shideh and she'll talk to Zari?

NAZANIN. You talk to Shideh?

SALME. I try to. Hey, when Shideh's back, let's go up to *shomal*. Mammad's khale has a villa up there. We'll be near water –

NAZANIN. I don't understand the point of *shomal* anymore now that we're covering.

SALME. But it's – it's still pretty.

NAZANIN. Can you do my leg, please?

(**SALME** *prepares the wax strip.*)

(**NAZANIN** *pets* **SALME***'s smooth arms.*)

Are you sure you don't wax your arms?

SALME. I'm too weak to wax anything.

NAZANIN. They're so smooth. My bush is out of control. Snagged the zipper of my pants yesterday.

SALME. Oh god.

NAZANIN. Do you even have a bush, Salme? I imagine your pussy is just like. A slab of marble.

(*Beat.*)

Pussy.

SALME. What?

NAZANIN. If I'm not the one to say it, I'll never hear it again, will I?

SALME. I can talk about my pussy.

NAZANIN. No. I. I don't know why it feels like you make fewer pussy jokes now.

SALME. I never really did.

NAZANIN. No, you did –

SALME. I always laughed! I still laugh! But I was never... the instigator of the pussy joke.

NAZANIN. Oh.

SALME. Am I boring you?

NAZANIN. What? No. Nono I'm. Uh.

I feel foggy?

SALME. Foggy?

NAZANIN. Foggy like...

> (**NAZANIN** *makes vague foggy motions.*)
>
> (**SALME** *mimics her.*)

SALME. Yeah.

> (**SALME** *looks at the mannequin.*)

That dress is so pretty.

NAZANIN. It's fine for now. Keeps me busy at least.

SALME. If the universities don't reopen for another year –

NAZANIN. I should – abandon years of education to what? Be a crappy seamstress?

SALME. No –

NAZANIN. Sometimes it feels like

my life is going sideways and

yours isn't.

You weren't in school when –

SALME. I'm gonna tell you something but you can't ask me how I know.

NAZANIN. Okay.

SALME. I know you were at the embassy.

The French one, I believe?

That's the only one left. I guess.

The other one is. Slightly occupied. Haha.

No, it's not funny.

NAZANIN. I don't even remember driving there. The line closed when I was third from the door. And I just felt. Relieved.

SALME. If you want to go back, I can. Go with you or.

NAZANIN. Why don't I want to leave?

SALME. We're not the only ones.

NAZANIN. I guess.

SALME. What am I thinking?

NAZANIN. What?

Oh.

SALME. One.

NAZANIN. Two.

SALME.	**NAZANIN.**
Pussy.	Car accidents.

NAZANIN. Oh.

SALME. Just a big, huge pussy.

NAZANIN. That's great.

SALME. A pussy so big – it's so big.

NAZANIN. Yeah. You got it.

SALME. Pussies that are um, growing from trees – I guess like a pussy tree –

NAZANIN. I have to pee.

> (**NAZANIN** *exits.* **SALME** *looks very alone. When* **NAZANIN** *returns:*)

Let's do it.

(SALME stares at the strip.)

You understand that it's more painful for me to do it, right?

SALME. No, I know.

(Beat.)

I'm sorry that I'm not. Mean.

NAZANIN. It's okay.

(Beat.)

I don't know if you're still doing this but

you can go ahead and put in your husband prayer for me.

If it's not too much trouble.

(NAZANIN tears the strip herself.)

5: Nazanin's Wedding

(1982.)

*(**NAZANIN**'s wedding day is here!)*

*(And four **WOMEN** are in the room!)*

*(No **RANA**. But everyone else!)*

*(**NAZANIN** is in her own version of the massive wedding dress.)*

*(**SALME** is doing **NAZANIN**'s hair.)*

*(**SHIDEH** is fussing with **NAZANIN**'s makeup.)*

*(**ZARI** is trying to find music on the radio.)*

SHIDEH. Someone's smelling fresh in here.

ZARI.	**SALME.**
Sorry.	Will you give me another one?

SHIDEH.	**NAZANIN.**
It might be me. I smell like an airplane.	Big or small?

ZARI.	**SALME.**
I can't find anything good on here.	Um.

SHIDEH.	**NAZANIN.**
Stop looking. It's illegal.	Here's one of each.

ZARI. Sometimes you can find something.

NAZANIN. Keep looking. You never know.

*(**SHIDEH** strokes **NAZANIN**'s "unibrow.")*

SHIDEH. Mother of god. Do you feel that, Nazanin? That right there is a unibrow.

NAZANIN. It's great to have you back, Shideh.

SHIDEH.	**ZARI.**
That's some thick hair you got.	Oh! Ohnevermind.

SALME. She doesn't have a unibrow.

SHIDEH. Right. Okay. So all this is just. A trick of the light.

NAZANIN. How much makeup are you putting on me, exactly?

SHIDEH. This is your wedding day.

NAZANIN. So?

SHIDEH. So you're not necessarily supposed to look like a person.

SALME. Do you want to eat something?

NAZANIN. Not hungry.

SALME.	**ZARI.**
Have a little bite.	I'm starving.

NAZANIN. Take it, Zari.

SHIDEH. Do not take the bride's food.

NAZANIN. Take it.

SHIDEH. Don't you dare take it.

ZARI. I'm taking it. Thank you, *aroos khanoom.*

NAZANIN. *Nooshi jaanet.*

(*NAZANIN nods.*)

(*ZARI gazes at her.*)

Oh god, what are you looking at?

Is it the dress? The dress is amazing. It makes me look simultaneously eighteen and sixty-five.

ZARI. No! No. You look – you're so pretty.

NAZANIN. Oh. Thanks.

ZARI. It's just, you know, it's – you're in a wedding dress!

NAZANIN. I know.

ZARI. In a good way!

NAZANIN. Yes, it's good.

> (**NAZANIN** *clears her throat.*)
>
> (*It draws a lot of attention.*)

ZARI. Are you excited to meet his dick tonight?

SHIDEH. Oh my god.

ZARI. I bet it's excited to meet you!

SHIDEH. What is *wrong* with you? *Zahre maar* –

ZARI.

Are you gonna have dinner with it?	**SHIDEH.**
Get your napkin ready.	...What does that even mean?
	Why would she need a napkin?

> (**ZARI** *whips around the napkin.*)

ZARI. But actually, he's really handsome, Nazy.

SHIDEH. Gorgeous. Strong hairline. That thing's not going anywhere.

NAZANIN. And his family / is –

ZARI. Good, good family.

SHIDEH. Family is so important.

ZARI. And a decent mother-in-law?

SHIDEH. I mean hello because we all know that Zari's
mother-in-law –

ZARI. Oh my god.

SHIDEH. Is a heinous woman.

ZARI. Mhm.

SHIDEH. Who belongs far away from human civilization.

NAZANIN. Did you see this watch? His mom bought it for
me.

SHIDEH.	ZARI.
She has great taste.	*Great* taste.

NAZANIN. She's a really good woman.

SHIDEH. What more could you want?

NAZANIN. Nothing, I guess.

>   *(Beat.)*

Sorry.

SHIDEH. What?

NAZANIN. My stomach.

SHIDEH. Are you / hungry?

>   *(Music plays from the radio.*)*

ZARI. Oh my god!

>   *(The* **WOMEN** *celebrate.)*

SHIDEH. Should we turn it / down?

---

*A license to produce *Wish You Were Here* does not include a performance
license for any third-party or copyrighted music. Licensees should create
an original composition or use music in the public domain. For further
information, please see the Music and Third-Party Materials Use Note
on page iii.

ZARI. Shideh!

SHIDEH. No.

ZARI. Shideh!

SHIDEH. No.

ZARI. Shideh!

SHIDEH. No.

ZARI. *Shideh bayad beraghseh!*

ALL. *Shideh bayad beraghseh!*

> (**SHIDEH** *dances with* **ZARI.**)

ZARI. Okay hold on who am I?

> (**ZARI** *dances like* **SALME,** *arms outstretched and swooping like a bird in flight.*)

NAZANIN.   **OTHERS.**
Salme Salme Salme –   Salme!

> (**ZARI** *flaps her wings across the room.*)

ZARI. Salme, you're a bird! You're a bird who got invited to a wedding! Okay my arms are getting tired *aroos bayad beraghseh!*

ALL. *Aroos bayad beraghseh! Aroos bayad beraghseh!*

> (**NAZANIN** *dances for a moment before the music cuts out.*)

ZARI. Come on.

NAZANIN. It's fine. It's fine. Zari, can you bring the fan over?

> (**ZARI** *brings the fan closer.*)

ZARI. Blink if you want a pussy audit.

SHIDEH. Don't. Nazy's older now. That thing is not so fresh.

NAZANIN. The day goes by fast, doesn't it?

ZARI. So fast. Incredibly fast.

SHIDEH. And you're gonna make so much money tonight, Nazanin.

NAZANIN. Not like we'll ever recoup the cost of the wedding –

SHIDEH. Wait until you see your gifts.

ZARI. I got a plate with Jimmy Carter's face on it.

SHIDEH. It's exquisite.

SALME. Do you not want to do this?

(*A terrible silence.*)

NAZANIN. Excuse me?

You're the one who prayed for this.

SALME. I can pray for something else to happen. Do you want me to / do that?

NAZANIN. No. Why would you even –

(*Beat.*)

I...hah.

I um,

thought I might

fall in love in my life.

Even if I never married I still thought

that was something

I would experience.

I mean, I'm not stupid.

Marriage is built on something different than...

it's a different kind of love, which I respect.

But doesn't everyone get to have that. Even briefly?

Why did I think I was promised that?

(*Beat.*)

SALME. That can still happen. You're growing old with this / person –

NAZANIN. I know, I know.

SALME. Your love doesn't reach its greatest heights today. It shouldn't.

NAZANIN. Alrightalright.

SALME. Trust me. I was so freaked out –

NAZANIN. I wish I hadn't said anything.

SHIDEH. Do you want me to find your mom?

NAZANIN. *No* god / no –

SHIDEH. I'm not scared of her.

NAZANIN. Great, now everyone's worried –

SHIDEH. Here are a few options: we can pretend you got hit by a car.

Zari can actually hit you with a car, can't you, Zari?

NAZANIN. Shideh, I'm fine. I don't want to get hit by a car today.

SHIDEH. Or *or* you can hit *me* with a car. Do you want to / do that?

ZARI. She's fine. / She's fine!

SHIDEH. Actually now that I say it out loud it's – you can hit me but you'd probably still have to go to your wedding –

ZARI. Give me your keys.

NAZANIN. My god. Indiana has changed you.

(*Beat.*)

SHIDEH. Nazy.

NAZANIN. What.

(*Beat.*)

SHIDEH. Can I eat some of that?

NAZANIN. Please.

SHIDEH. I'm jet-lagged and hungry.

NAZANIN. Finish it. I think we're done here.

SALME. Do you like it?

NAZANIN. It's fine.

SALME. We can re-do it. I want you to love your wedding photographs. You might want to – you might –

NAZANIN. I might what?

SALME. Nothing.

NAZANIN. If you say my children –

SALME. I didn't say it.

NAZANIN. You can't *say* things like that.

SALME. I didn't say it.

NAZANIN. You thought it.

SALME. You don't have to have children –

NAZANIN. You said I'd get married, now I'm getting married. Now the children. You keep speaking these *things* into existence andand Zari wants children so why don't you work your magic on her uterus.

SHIDEH. Salme. Do not mentally inseminate Zari until she has a green card.

NAZANIN. You're applying for a green card?

ZARI. Jamshid's father is applying for us. Just to be safe.

NAZANIN. That's really smart.

SHIDEH. We'll be roommates!

NAZANIN. Where's Jamshid gonna live?

SHIDEH. Oh wow god I wonder hm let me just *I do not give a shit.*

ZARI. It's probably not gonna happen and I don't even know if I want to go –

NAZANIN. I'm happy for you. I hope you get it.

ZARI. Thank you.

    (Beat.)

SHIDEH. *Aroos khanoom.*

NAZANIN. Mhm.

SHIDEH. This is a good thing.

NAZANIN. Yeah.

SHIDEH. Even if you get divorced.

NAZANIN. Okay.

SHIDEH. And everyone starts treating you like a whore.

NAZANIN. Mhm.

SHIDEH. *(Getting emotional.)* I think you look really beautiful today.

SALME.	**NAZANIN.**
Doesn't she?	Shideh, why don't you lie down?

SHIDEH. I was in the middle seat and I didn't have an armrest. Sorry.

NAZANIN. Okay, let's do this.

ZARI. I'll call the cab.

SALME. Shoot. Can we – five minutes – it's noon –

NAZANIN. Salme.

SALME. Five minutes.

NAZANIN. It's never five minutes.

SHIDEH. The driver won't be here for another ten –

NAZANIN. No. She has to wash. She has to pray. For everyone! And everything!

And I want to go. If we don't go now – not today, Salme.

SHIDEH. We can go separately –

NAZANIN. I want a day without your prayers. Can that be my gift?

　　　　　(Beat.)

SALME. Of course. No, I'm sorry. Let's go.

6: Two Again

(1983.)

(Just two now: **NAZANIN** *and* **ZARI**.)

(They are both dressed in black formal clothing.)

(**NAZANIN** *wears her roosari and manteau;* **ZARI** *does not.)*

(**ZARI** *flips through a Quran.)*

ZARI. People can actually read this, you know?

NAZANIN. The Quran?

ZARI. There are little boys in Tajikistan who can't spell their name but can recite this whole thing.

NAZANIN. Yeah.

ZARI. That's crazy.

NAZANIN. How.

ZARI. What do you mean?

NAZANIN. What do *you* mean?

ZARI. It's intense.

NAZANIN. Do you not think you're Muslim?

ZARI. No, I am, but I'm, you know, not as Muslim as the little boys who recite this front to back.

NAZANIN. Is there something wrong with being very Muslim?

ZARI. No! I guess I didn't think of us as very devout. That's all.

NAZANIN. Do you think that I don't believe in God?

ZARI. That's different than...all of this.

NAZANIN. Put that down. She really believed in all that and you're holding it like it's a a a put it down.

(**ZARI** *gently sets the Quran down.*)

Do you have the number for the cab company –

ZARI. I thought we could be here for a little. If you can.

(**NAZANIN** *takes a second. Then takes off her roosari and manteau.*)

(*But still doesn't settle in.*)

NAZANIN. Yeah, okay.

ZARI. When's the last time you were here?

NAZANIN. Not sure.

ZARI. It's been awhile. I'm happy you're here.

Okay, we have *sharbat*, chai, but it's a little hot / for chai –

NAZANIN. I don't want anything. My stomach aches.

ZARI. I grow mint now! By the window! Give me one minute.

NAZANIN. No, it's the heat.

ZARI. Well, *sharbat* can't hurt.

(**ZARI** *waits out* **NAZANIN.**)

(**NAZANIN** *rolls her eyes.*)

Yeah, I. I'll be right back.

(**ZARI** *exits then enters with two glasses of sharbat.*)

Can I interest you in a / straw?

NAZANIN. Are you happy or something?

ZARI. What? No.

NAZANIN. Where are your coasters? Do you not have coasters?

ZARI. I think they're in a drawer –

NAZANIN. Nevermind.

ZARI. I wish you would drink that. It was really hot in the *masjid*.

Felt like it was hotter in the *masjid*, actually –

NAZANIN. You know what, I can probably catch a cab outside.

ZARI. Oh, okay.

> (**NAZANIN** *shoots up.*)
>
> (*A spot of blood has bloomed where she was sitting.*)
>
> (**ZARI** *sees the blood.*)

Oh. Uh.

NAZANIN. What?

ZARI. Nothing, nothing, let's go –

NAZANIN. Oh my god are you kidding me – Was that me –

ZARI. Nono. The couch just does that sometimes.

NAZANIN. Shit.

ZARI. Look at you! A day-one bleeder! Very impressive.

NAZANIN. Sorry.

ZARI. Oh, man. That's good. Give me one second.

> (**ZARI** *exits, still laughing, and returns with clothes for* **NAZANIN.**)

I think these will fit you.

NAZANIN. Sorry.

       *(**NAZANIN** exits.)*

       *(**ZARI** gets cleaning supplies and cleans the spot.)*

       *(**NAZANIN** returns in **ZARI**'s pants.)*

Stop cleaning that.

ZARI. Did you find the pads?

NAZANIN. That won't leave a spot, will it?

ZARI. Not if you catch it early. Please sit down.

       *(**NAZANIN** sits.)*

Are you ever gonna tell me how it happened?

NAZANIN. I wish you'd have pieced it together. Or asked someone else.

ZARI. Who would I have asked but you –

NAZANIN. Why do you need / to know now?

ZARI. If she were here, she would tell me. And she would never make me feel like shit about asking.

       (Beat.)

NAZANIN. She and Mammad –

Well, Mammad's *khale* has a villa in *shomal*.

And she kept badgering me to go.

Anyway, they went, just the two of them.

And she went swimming.

And now that I think of it, I don't ever remember seeing Salme swim.

ZARI. Was there

a strong tide or

how did...

NAZANIN. I didn't want to ask. But.

If she was swimming, then she was in the water with her *manteau*, and her hijab and...

You can't... You're not supposed to swim in all that.

(*Beat.*)

How fucking stupid is that.

ZARI. Oh my god. Nazy. I'm so / sorry –

NAZANIN. She was the only one who looked for Rana.

She's the only one who calls Shideh.

ZARI. I call / Shideh sometimes.

NAZANIN. And she never stopped calling you.

Even when you stopped answering.

So I wonder. Where we all go now that there's no one to locate us.

(*Beat.*)

ZARI. I should call Shideh more.

And I'll keep looking for Rana. If you want me to.

I called two of her classmates when she first – you know. I can call them / again –

NAZANIN. You made two calls. You didn't try.

ZARI. Nazanin, you didn't call anyone.

(**NAZANIN** *gathers her things.*)

NAZANIN. *Bebin*, I'm tired. And I know it's like 100 degrees outside but your hair smells so bad. And I might vomit on your nice furniture, which I have already ruined, so best to excuse myself now.

ZARI. Okay so I'm a person and my hair sweats in heat like a person –

NAZANIN. That's not sweat. That's scalp. Wash your hair.

ZARI. I do wash my hair.

NAZANIN. Obviously not every day.

ZARI. No one should wash their hair every day.

NAZANIN. You should.

ZARI. That's propaganda and I won't do it. Stop it. Stop rolling your eyes. You are not allowed to roll your eyes at people in front of them.

NAZANIN. Well –

ZARI. You have a way of making me feel really lonely.

NAZANIN. I don't mean to.

ZARI. Yes, you do. You love it.

    (Beat.)

NAZANIN. Was I like this with Salme?

I was, wasn't I?

ZARI. Yes.

NAZANIN. I um.

I wonder if anyone will ever love me like that again.

Rana didn't...

    (Beat.)

ZARI. I...

NAZANIN. What?

ZARI. I was about to apologize to you for being the only one left.

I can't even tell – whether you don't like me anymore or if you never really liked me.

But I think it's time we made a decision.

Because there's no way you enjoy this.

And when I'm with you, I wish I were alone and...

NAZANIN. Yeah.

ZARI. And you were – you were *so* territorial with Salme.

You claimed her. But she wasn't yours.

NAZANIN. I know.

ZARI. And all I can think about today is how she loved you more than she loved me.

  (Beat.)

NAZANIN. I guess it doesn't – you'll end up getting your green card and –

ZARI. I'm not leaving.

  (Beat.)

NAZANIN. Does Shideh know?

ZARI. She's in exams. We called her mom. We're waiting another month to tell her.

I hope that's – I hope she doesn't end up hating me for that.

NAZANIN. She won't.

  (Beat.)

ZARI. I'll drive you home.

NAZANIN. Do you think it's my / fault?

ZARI. No.

NAZANIN. But listen.

ZARI. It's just not.

NAZANIN. Everyone who loves me feels alone.

(*Beat.*)

ZARI. Maybe you don't remember.

But we used to be friends.

You used to really like me.

NAZANIN. I remember.

(**ZARI** *turns the TV on.*)

Can I ask you a favor?

ZARI. Yeah.

NAZANIN. If you leave, don't tell me.

I don't want to know.

Do you promise?

ZARI. Yes.

NAZANIN. Thank you.

7: You & I

(1984.)

(Something like a baby shower has just ended.)

(A small pile of gifts sits on the table.)

(A very pregnant **NAZANIN** *lies on the couch as* **ZARI** *shaves* **NAZANIN**'s *legs.)*

ZARI. Don't think about it.

NAZANIN. That was so mean.

ZARI. I know.

NAZANIN. Everyone has spider veins.

ZARI. Everyone!

NAZANIN. Even if I wasn't / pregnant –

ZARI. She had no right to say that to you.

To talk about your body critically in front of you.

That's for you to do privately in your own head.

NAZANIN. I hate women.

ZARI. She's a rotten-egg bitch with a rotten-egg pussy. And that's that.

NAZANIN. Thank you.

ZARI. What'd she get you? The pacifier set?

NAZANIN. No. It was. The um. The bag over there. Can I see it?

ZARI. I'm sure it's tacky, ugly, and cheap, but let's see.

(ZARI hands NAZANIN the gift.)

(NAZANIN begins to open it.)

NAZANIN. I would never say something like that. I mean. Isn't there a code of etiquette? Don't people know not to say those kinds of things to *oh that's so cute* –

ZARI. Oh my god. Oh my god –

NAZANIN. So *kuchulu*!

ZARI. Shit. You have to call her. Yeah.

NAZANIN. Dammit.

ZARI. Bitches have good taste sometimes. It's unfortunate but it happens.

NAZANIN. I hate that.

ZARI. Nothing could be worse.

> (ZARI *shaves* NAZANIN*'s ankles with care.*)

The universities are re-opening.

NAZANIN. I heard. Are you going back?

ZARI. No. Are you?

NAZANIN. I would. But I probably can't anymore.

ZARI. Why not?

NAZANIN. You know.

ZARI. I don't know.

NAZANIN. How would they even – do our records even exist? I'm too old to take a placement exam.

ZARI. I'm not sure.

> (*Beat.*)

NAZANIN. Are you and Jamshid still...trying?

ZARI. We're taking a short break. From all that.

NAZANIN. Good idea.

ZARI. We have time.

NAZANIN. You have a lot of time. And if you really bond with this one, it's yours. But you'll have to pay for its nose job.

ZARI. I was already paying for its nose job. I've seen your cousins.

NAZANIN. Yeah, it's pretty bad.

ZARI. And I would like your child to have peripheral vision.

NAZANIN. Aw. That's sweet.

ZARI. You know, some part of me still thinks in one year, two things will – we'll return to some kind of normal. Am I an idiot?

NAZANIN. No. No.

> *(Beat.)*

Did you ever really see me doing this?

ZARI. No. But now that you are. It makes sense.

> *(Beat.)*

NAZANIN. I don't know that I'll ever get to be

who I wanted to be.

> *(Beat.)*

I used to think about it a lot.

ZARI. Do you think about it now?

NAZANIN. I don't not think about it.

But not a lot. Not all the time.

ZARI. What do you think about now?

NAZANIN. The very specific ways in which I will ruin this child.

ZARI. That's good!

NAZANIN. Yeah.

ZARI. Are you scared?

NAZANIN. Yeah. / You know.

ZARI. Of course.

NAZANIN. But also I'm. There's a terrifying part of me. That thinks I'll be good at this.

And Salme said I would do this.

I like thinking I'm who she thought I was.

ZARI. Yeah.

> *(Beat.)*

NAZANIN. And I don't mean it all like – *oh so sad* – I don't even remember what I wanted to be –

ZARI. You could have been anything.

NAZANIN. Oh, I don't / know.

ZARI. Anything. Not that – sorry –

NAZANIN. Whatwhy?

ZARI. I'm talking about you like your life is over. It's not.

NAZANIN. But I. Thank you. For. Yeah.

> *(Beat.)*

Do you love me enough to give me a bikini wax?

ZARI. I would give anyone a bikini wax.

NAZANIN. Rana once tried to wax me down there but she got the wax too close to my, you know, like, the parts of your vagina where hair can't even grow.

ZARI. Oh god. Oh god.

NAZANIN. And for the first time in my life, I heard my vagina scream.

ZARI. No. No no no no no no –

NAZANIN. No itit was –

ZARI. Can I say something?

NAZANIN. Zari, just laugh. I didn't tell the story right.

ZARI. She wasn't that nice.

NAZANIN. Rana?

ZARI. Yes.

NAZANIN. She was. Nice to me.

ZARI. She loved you and Salme. I shrunk around her.

NAZANIN. Sometimes I wonder if I made her up.

ZARI. Do you hate her?

NAZANIN. I can't really decide.

ZARI. I can always hate her for you. Until you don't want to anymore.

>   (**ZARI** *joins* **NAZANIN** *on the couch.*)

>   (*They lie together, head-to-head.*)

NAZANIN. I love you more.

ZARI. That's not what I meant.

NAZANIN. And I wish I'd looked for her, because I want you to know I'd look for you.

ZARI. Do you love me because I'm the only one left?

NAZANIN. No. God no.

ZARI. Why does everyone care so much about voting?

>   (**NAZANIN** *laughs.*)

No, I know. I don't mean that.

NAZANIN. I know exactly what you mean. I mean it, too.

(Beat.)

ZARI. God, I used to be so dumb. I would give anything to feel dumb again.

NAZANIN. You weren't dumb.

ZARI. I wonder if I will ever feel like that again. Like I'm floating.

NAZANIN. You're still floating.

Look, we're floating.

(Beat.)

Even if I did love you because you're the only one left...

I don't but – I don't think that would be a terrible reason to love someone.

ZARI. I don't either.

8: Two Become One

(1985.)

(ZARI repeatedly knocks from outside the front door.)

(She barges in, in full hijab.)

(NAZANIN is not onstage.)

(The dress on the mannequin is almost finished.)

ZARI. Nazanin?

Nazanin?

NAZANIN.

(NAZANIN enters.)

NAZANIN. *(Startled.)* Oh my god.

ZARI. I've been calling you nonstop.

NAZANIN. I unplugged the phone.

ZARI. Why?

NAZANIN. The baby's down. Good news?

ZARI. *(Stepping on a toy.)* Oh no *ow.*

NAZANIN. Oh sorry. Here, *roosari-to bede* –

ZARI. No, I'll keep / it –

NAZANIN. Aren't you staying?

ZARI. Can I put it here?

NAZANIN. Are you okay?

ZARI. Yeah!

NAZANIN. Okay...give me a second.

(**NAZANIN** *leaves to change.*)

(*Offstage.*) I might be allergic to my lotion.

It has fragrance in it.

Are you sensitive to fragrance?

Zari?

ZARI. What?

(**NAZANIN** *returns, dressed.*)

NAZANIN. Nothing, nevermind.

ZARI. No, what'd you ask?

NAZANIN. It literally doesn't matter.

ZARI. I want to know.

NAZANIN. I asked if your lotion makes you itchy.

ZARI. Oh. Um. No.

NAZANIN. Great. Do you want chai / or *sharbat*?

ZARI. I need nail polish.

NAZANIN. Nail polish?

ZARI. Yes.

NAZANIN. What color?

ZARI. What do you think?

NAZANIN. Um. Red always looks nice on you.

ZARI. Let's do red.

(**NAZANIN** *retrieves her nail-polish bag.*)

(*A car honks from outside.*)

NAZANIN. Obnoxious.

ZARI. Will you do my nails?

NAZANIN. Will you sit down now?

ZARI. Yes.

    (They sit down.)

    *(***NAZANIN*** paints ***ZARI****'s nails.)*

Did you ever play the piano?

NAZANIN. No. You didn't, right?

ZARI. No.

NAZANIN. A cockroach flew out of the vent yesterday. Should I move?

ZARI. Yes.

NAZANIN. Hey, Shideh's not engaged, right?

ZARI. No. Why do you ask?

NAZANIN. I'm looking for a pediatrician. Shideh's not studying to be a pediatrician, is she?

ZARI. No. I do not think she works with children.

NAZANIN. That would be scary.

ZARI. But she has a boyfriend!

NAZANIN. Oh!

ZARI. He's Puerto Rican. Or Polish? It was a P sound. He's missing his two bottom canines. Isn't that cool?

NAZANIN. That is cool.

ZARI. You should call her. She would love that.

NAZANIN. I'm so bad at all that.

    (Beat.)

No judging.

ZARI. No judging.

NAZANIN. Salme's prayer rug is still here. And I know I should give it to her parents.

ZARI. It should be yours.

NAZANIN. I found a little prayer stone, too. It must be hers.

ZARI. Yeah.

NAZANIN. Do you want it?

ZARI. I mean, would you –

NAZANIN. Of course. Of course you should have it.

(**NAZANIN** *places it next to* **ZARI**.)

ZARI. Nazy, how did we first meet?

NAZANIN. Oh. Hm.

ZARI. I couldn't really. Think of how.

NAZANIN. God, I don't know.

ZARI. I wish I remembered.

NAZANIN. One day we just knew each other.

(*Another honk from outside.*)

You can't just *honk* like that – I have a napping baby –

ZARI. It's my cab. I'm so sorry.

NAZANIN. Where's your car?

ZARI. In the shop. Let it wait let it wait –

NAZANIN. Zari –

ZARI. What am I thinking? One.

(*Beat.*)

One.

(*Beat.*)

NAZANIN. Two.

NAZANIN.
    Mulberry trees.
	ZARI.
	    Wedding veils.

NAZANIN. Oh.

ZARI. One.

NAZANIN. Two.

NAZANIN.
    Honey.
	ZARI.
	    Honey.

    (Beat.)

NAZANIN. Honey. Yeah.

ZARI. I know I *know* you didn't want me to tell you but –

    (Beat.)

I just. Didn't think. That you really.

    (Beat.)

NAZANIN. Your cab is waiting. You can go.

ZARI. I'm going to call you.

NAZANIN. If your cab wakes up my baby –

ZARI. I didn't want to do it like Rana –

NAZANIN. Well maybe she had the right idea *I said I didn't want to know.*

ZARI. I can sponsor you, if you apply for a visa –

NAZANIN. If you don't leave in ten seconds, I'm calling the police.

I'll tell them there's whiskey and records and and whatever in your house.

I'm calling the police.

(**ZARI** *stands there.*)

(*Neither of them move.*)

(*Until* **ZARI** *picks up Salme's prayer stone.*)

(*Re: prayer stone.*) No. *No.* She loved me more than she loved you.

(**ZARI** *sets the prayer stone back down before leaving.*)

(**NAZANIN** *stands there in the ugly wake of all that.*)

(*Nothing happens for a long time.*)

(*Then the baby starts crying.*)

(*Time moves around her.*)

(*Time is moving. She is not.*)

(*We go from 1986 to 1987 to 1988 to 1989 to 1990.*)

9: New Friends

(1990.)

*(**NAZANIN** is taking a **NEW FRIEND**'s coat and roosari.)*

(A mannequin with pieces of a dress pinned onto it stands somewhere.)

*(**NAZANIN** throws house sandals at the **WOMAN**'s feet.)*

NAZANIN. *Befarmayid.*

NEW FRIEND. *Mamnoonam.*

NAZANIN. Please, please.

NEW FRIEND. My car has / no fan.

NAZANIN. I'm glad I saw you. You shouldn't be waiting in your car.

NEW FRIEND. I appreciate it, Nasrin *khanoom* –

NAZANIN. My name is Nazanin. / *Befarmayid, befarmayid.*

NEW FRIEND. I'm so sorry – Thank you.

Wow, I. Oh, right, you're a designer.

NAZANIN. I'm a seamstress. Not a designer.

NEW FRIEND. Oh, okay.

NAZANIN. This is hideous. I would never design this.

NEW FRIEND. No, it's – you're artsy.

NAZANIN. No. I'm good at the – putting it together stuff.

I was studying to be an engineer before the – it doesn't matter.

NEW FRIEND. What kind of engineer?

NAZANIN. Civil.

NEW FRIEND. *(Motioning to herself.)* Mechanical.

> *(Beat.)*

NAZANIN. The boys are getting popsicles. Right around the corner.

NEW FRIEND. Let me – how much –

NAZANIN. Please don't.

NEW FRIEND. I must.

NAZANIN. *Tarof nadaram.*

NEW FRIEND. I can't let you –

NAZANIN. Yes, you can.

NEW FRIEND. Please.

NAZANIN. If you pay me, I'll throw myself out the window. Won't you sit?

NEW FRIEND. Thank you.

NAZANIN. *Rahat baash.* It's too warm for chai, isn't it?

NEW FRIEND. Sit. Please. I don't need anything.

NAZANIN. I would offer you *sharbat* but we just ran out.

NEW FRIEND. I don't like *sharbat*. Not to be rude – it's so sweet.

NAZANIN. I don't like it either.

NEW FRIEND. Gives me a tension headache.

NAZANIN. Me too. Bad memories.

> *(**NAZANIN** fetches water and serves **NEW FRIEND**.)*
>
> *(Then she hovers over her and offers her fruit.)*

NAZANIN. Please eat something.

NEW FRIEND. No thank you.

NAZANIN. Please, my back is hurting. Take something.

NEW FRIEND. *Dastet dard nakoneh.*

NAZANIN. They'll be back any second now. With the –

NEW FRIEND. With the popsicles.

NAZANIN. The snowman ones. Those are the ones they're looking for.

> (**NEW FRIEND** *takes a cucumber.*)

You studied mechanical?

NEW FRIEND. Mhm.

NAZANIN. But what do you do now?

NEW FRIEND. I'm a mechanical. Engineer.

NAZANIN. You work as an engineer?

NEW FRIEND. I went back to school.

NAZANIN. Good for you.

I didn't.

NEW FRIEND. I almost didn't. But then I did.

It's never too late.

NAZANIN. It's definitely too late.

> (*They sip their water.*)
>
> (**NEW FRIEND** *nibbles on the cucumber.*)
>
> (*It's like this for a little bit.*)

NEW FRIEND. You know, if I drive up the street, I can catch them now.

NAZANIN. Probably. Yeah.

(NEW FRIEND rises from her seat.)

(She gasps in horror.)

(She has perioded on the couch.)

NEW FRIEND. Oh my god.

NAZANIN. What?

NEW FRIEND. Um.

NAZANIN. Oh. Oh shit.

Uh.

The bathroom

is the second door on the left.

There are – pads under the sink.

Oh, you'll probably need...

Do you think you'll need...underwear?

I – yes, I think you will.

One second.

> *(She quietly exits and returns with spare pants, underwear, and a pad.)*

Here.

NEW FRIEND. Thank you.

> *(NEW FRIEND exits.)*

> *(NAZANIN cleans the blood.)*

> *(NEW FRIEND returns in NAZANIN's clothes.)*

I beg you to let me clean that.

NAZANIN. It lifts easily if it doesn't sit.

NEW FRIEND. Thank god.

I'm going to give you just a little bit for / the –

NAZANIN. Listen, honestly, I'm not replacing the cushion.

NEW FRIEND. Please let me give you money.

NAZANIN. No.

NEW FRIEND. Let me clean that.

NAZANIN. It's fine.

NEW FRIEND. Here's all the money in my purse.

NAZANIN. My Turkish soap is about to come on so could you just sit. Please.

>   (**NEW FRIEND** *sits.*)

>   (**NAZANIN** *turns on the TV.*)

Do you want – nevermind. Nevermind.

>   (*Beat.*)

Listen, I know – I can change it.

NEW FRIEND. Don't.

NAZANIN. I know it's objectively bad.

NEW FRIEND. This is an excellent show.

NAZANIN. My husband doesn't –

NEW FRIEND. It's not for men.

NAZANIN. Right.

>   (*Beat.*)

NEW FRIEND. Funny to have lived through a war and still be mortified by your own period.

NAZANIN. Yeah.

>   (*Beat.*)

So you never left?

NEW FRIEND. I tried. I visited the States briefly.

NAZANIN. Where?

NEW FRIEND. New York. The state not the city.

I knew I couldn't do it.

I guess it's just me.

That stain is going to come out, right?

NAZANIN. Yes.

NEW FRIEND. If I come back and there is a spot –

NAZANIN. What if you come back and there's a new couch –

NEW FRIEND. I would finally leave the country.

    (Beat.)

NAZANIN. I could never leave. I love being from somewhere beautiful.

NEW FRIEND. Not everyone gets to be from somewhere beautiful.

NAZANIN. And more of us stayed than left. We're in the majority.

NEW FRIEND. I guess.

Makes me feel

so sad for them.

NAZANIN. I don't feel sorry for them.

I mostly feel this like

thing in my throat

and when it rises

the rest of the day feels long.

NEW FRIEND. Well, you should.

NAZANIN. Be angry?

NEW FRIEND. Feel sorry for them.

(*Beat.*)

NEW FRIEND. They're castaways.

NAZANIN. Oh.

(*Beat.*)

NEW FRIEND. It's a terrible thing, isn't it?

10: A Phone Call

(1991.)

*(**NAZANIN** cleans her home.)*

(She sweeps under the rug.)

(She finds a dead cockroach and attempts to sweep it out.)

(The telephone rings, but she doesn't pick it up.)

(The telephone stops ringing.)

(It rings again, but she is still busy with the cockroach.)

(It stops ringing.)

(Finally, she sweeps the cockroach out.)

(The telephone rings again.)

(This time, she answers it on speakerphone.)

*(She hears **RANA**'s voice on the other line.)*

NAZANIN. *Allo?*

Allo salaam?

RANA. Nazanin?

NAZANIN. *Balleh?*

RANA. I'm sorry. May I speak to Nazanin?

NAZANIN. This is Nazanin. May I ask who's calling?

(Beat.)

Hello? Hello?

Can I help you?

(**RANA** *laughs.*)

(**NAZANIN** *recognizes her laugh, panics, and hangs up the phone.*)

(*She stands in the wake of that for a few moments.*)

(*Then panics even harder.*)

NAZANIN. Oh my god *fuck.*

(*She picks the receiver back up.*)

Rana? Rana? Hello?

Shit. Oh my god. Shit.

(*She fumbles with the phone, trying to call Rana back, but absolutely not knowing how.*)

(*She starts breathing heavily, on the verge of tears.*)

(*She puts the phone down. Maybe it's better if it's on the receiver? She stares at the phone. Waiting, waiting, waiting. But nothing.*)

(*She drops to the floor and stays there for a long time.*)

(*Then she has a vision of* **SALME**, **ZARI**, *and* **SHIDEH**.)

(**NAZANIN** *stares at this vision of* **SALME**.)

(*The telephone rings.*)

(*This time,* **NAZANIN** *lunges toward it.*)

(**RANA** *appears.*)

Rana?

RANA. Nazanin?

NAZANIN. Yeah. That's. It's me.

RANA. Hi.

NAZANIN. Hi.

> *(Beat.)*

RANA. Did you hang up on me?

NAZANIN. Yes.

RANA. Okay. That was mean.

> *(***NAZANIN** *laughs.)*

> *(They breathe on the phone for a few moments.)*

What are you doing?

NAZANIN. What do you mean?

RANA. What were you doing just now?

NAZANIN. I guess I was praying.

> *(***RANA** *laughs.)*

> *(***NAZANIN** *laughs, too.)*

RANA. Are you a big Muslim now?

NAZANIN. Are you still a big Jew?

RANA. I am.

NAZANIN. Well, *alhamdulillah.*

> *(When the laughter subsides:)*

RANA. Do you have children?

> *(***NAZANIN** *looks at the toys strewn about the home.)*

NAZANIN. No.

RANA. Wait, really?

NAZANIN. No. I don't.

RANA. Nazanin! Good for you!

NAZANIN. Thank you!

RANA. Do you want to ask me something?

NAZANIN. Yes, but – I just – I don't know I – *oh* where are you?!

RANA. San Jose.

NAZANIN. Where?

RANA. California.

NAZANIN. California? Los Angeles?

RANA. No. Closer to San Francisco.

But we'd like to move south. Los Angeles is south of San Jose.

What we want to do is join the masses in Orange County.

NAZANIN. We thought you were in Israel.

RANA. I was. For five years.

NAZANIN. We tried to find you. Well, Salme. Salme tried to...

   (Beat.)

RANA. She tried to find me?

NAZANIN. Yeah.

And I don't think

she ever stopped looking for you.

   (This is hugely beautiful to **RANA.***)*

RANA. Thank you for telling me that.

NAZANIN. Mhm.

RANA. How is Salme?

(*Beat.*)

NAZANIN. She's good.

She got highlights.

It suits her.

(*Beat.*)

What were you doing

yesterday

at three in the afternoon?

RANA. Working.

NAZANIN. Where? Where do you work?

RANA. I work at a tragic American pizza establishment.

NAZANIN. Pizza! I love pizza.

RANA. It's called Pizza Hut. It's not like Iranian pizza.

But I also get the feeling it's not like Italian pizza.

NAZANIN. Oh so is it like a cafe?

RANA. Mhm yeah it's a very special place.

NAZANIN. Do they only sell pizza?

RANA. No, there's pasta and salad. Things like that.

NAZANIN. Do you eat there?

RANA. Most nights.

NAZANIN. Lucky.

RANA. Okay so we get unlimited fountain sodas.

NAZANIN. So like Coke?

RANA. Like Pepsi. But it's the same thing. And. Okay. I fell in love with it because it's fucking delicious and I didn't touch a glass of water that whole winter and obviously, I got a kidney stone.

NAZANIN. Oh my god no.

RANA. I passed it.

NAZANIN. Good.

RANA. I was like, hovered over the toilet, screaming for mercy –

NAZANIN. Nononono –

RANA. And now I have ruined Pepsi for myself. Which is disappointing. Because it may have been my favorite thing about America.

NAZANIN. Uh, can I ask you

sort of a stupid question?

RANA. Go right ahead.

NAZANIN. Are you –

Do you –

Live there now?

Like, you're not.

Coming back.

RANA. Yeah, I. Guess I live here.

(Beat.)

You know, they're being more lenient with visa applications now.

So you could find your way over here someday. To see me.

NAZANIN. At the Pizza Hut cafe.

RANA. My treat.

   (Beat.)

RANA. You can meet my daughter.

NAZANIN. You have a daughter?

RANA. Soon. I found out officially last week but. I knew.

   (Beat.)

You know, I'm gonna. Have this girl.

I'm gonna move her to Orange County.

I'm gonna get her a dog.

She won't be scared of dogs like me.

I'm gonna make her pet every dog in the street because dogs are nice here.

She will have a home.

A home, one home.

I won't teach her Farsi.

She will never have to know what an F4 or an IR2 is.

She won't even know the world *revolution.*

Never.

Never.

She will never know how fast this earth can spin underneath you.

How one day you can have a home and the next

as you are hurtling through the air

you will have to vanquish home

the word home

the idea of home

as anything that has ever existed or will exist again.

All she will know is the calm

of a quiet, ordinary existence.

Because the ground underneath her feet is gonna be still.

So fucking still.

>*(Beat.)*

NAZANIN. Why didn't you call?

RANA. I thought you'd be mad at me.

Were you?

NAZANIN. No.

>*(Beat.)*

RANA. Even if you were, I want you to know that

when I think about where I'm from, I think of you.

>*(They can't think of anything else to stay.)*

>*(Every second that passes becomes unbearable.)*

NAZANIN. Being your best friend. Was my whole personality.

I miss it. I miss being defined by who you were.

In the long shadow of your existence, I found a home.

I could have stayed there forever.

I found a cockroach under the rug.

I wonder if it was here when you were here.

I should get going.

RANA. Okay.

NAZANIN. I mean you should – this call can't be cheap.

RANA. Yeah. I don't care –

NAZANIN. Wait *waitwait* –

RANA. I'm here.

NAZANIN. What's your phone number?

RANA. Do you have a pen?

NAZANIN. Yeah.

RANA. Okay it's. 4 0 8 – sorry, country code 1.

Yeah. 1. 4 0 8. 5 5 1. 0 5 6 8.

Will you read it back to me?

NAZANIN. Country code 1. 4 0 8 5 5 1 0 5 6 8.

RANA. That's it.

You should call me.

(Beat.)

Okay, Naz Banu. I hope you have a great day.

NAZANIN. And I hope you have a great...night.

RANA. I will.

NAZANIN. Sweet dreams.

RANA. Bye.

NAZANIN. Bye, Rana.

*(**NAZANIN** hangs up.)*

(She lets herself cry.)

(When it wanes, she sweeps up the roach and tosses it into the garbage.)

(She might still be softly crying as she does this.)

(She's probably muttering "gross" or "ew" as that happens.)

(She takes a breath. Redoes her ponytail. Blows her nose.)

(She rolls up the rug. Stores it.)

(Then continues to clean the room.)

End of Play